STREGA NONA
Her Story

as told to
Tomie dePaola

PUFFIN BOOKS

*For Connie, Mel, Tom, Alan, Jon, Gary, Wendy, Josette,
Julie, Mary L., Leif, Steve, Cary, Ricia, Mary G., Mary C.,
and all the others at The Children's Theatre Company in
Minneapolis, for helping bring Strega Nona and her
friends to life on the stage.*

PUFFIN BOOKS
Published by the Penguin Group
Penguin Putnam Books for Young Readers, 345 Hudson Street, New York, New York 10014, U.S.A.
Penguin Books Ltd, 27 Wrights Lane, London W8 5TZ, England
Penguin Books Australia Ltd, Ringwood, Victoria, Australia
Penguin Books Canada Ltd, 10 Alcorn Avenue, Toronto, Ontario, Canada M4V 3B2
Penguin Books (N.Z.) Ltd, 182-190 Wairau Road, Auckland 10, New Zealand

Penguin Books Ltd, Registered Offices: Harmondsworth, Middlesex, England

First published in the United States of America by G. P. Putnam's Sons,
a member of The Putnam & Grosset Group, 1996
Published by Puffin Books, a division of Penguin Putnam Books for Young Readers, 2000

14 16 18 20 19 17 15

Copyright © Tomie dePaola, 1996
All rights reserved

THE LIBRARY OF CONGRESS HAS CATALOGED THE G. P. PUTNAM'S SONS EDITION AS FOLLOWS:
dePaola, Tomie. Strega Nona: Her Story /
written and illustrated by Tomie dePaola. p. cm.
Summary: Grandma Concetta heals everyone with her remedies and advice, and
when she retires, she leaves Nona her magic pasta pot with its secret ingredient.
[1. Grandmothers—Fiction. 2. Magic—Fiction. 3. Healing—Fiction.] I. Title.
PZ7.D439Sq 1996 [E]—dc20 95-22824 CIP AC
ISBN 0-399-22818-7

This edition ISBN 0-698-11814-6

Printed in the United States of America

It all began one night a long time ago, in a little village in the hills of Calabria, in the country now known as Italy. Almost everyone was fast asleep.

The weather was fierce that dark night. The wind blew and blew. A cold rain fell. And a baby was about to be born.

"Oh, my poor wife," Giuseppe, the young husband, said to Zia Rosa, who was there to help. "Every child of ours was brought into the world by Grandma Concetta. But with this terrible weather, how will she be able to come down from her little house on the hill?"

Hours passed. The wind blew harder. More rain fell. Still the baby didn't come. "Where is that baby?" Giuseppe asked.

Zia Rosa lit a candle. "Perhaps it is waiting," she answered.

"For what?" Giuseppe asked.

"For ME!" cried Grandma Concetta, bursting through the doorway on a gust of wind. "No grandchild of mine can be born without ME!" Taking off her cloak and rolling up her sleeves, she headed for the bedroom. "Follow me, Rosa. Now the baby will come!"

And sure enough, a baby girl was born in no time at all.

"Ah," said Grandma Concetta, looking down at the new *bambina*,
"she shall be called Nona. And she will become a strega."

As soon as little Nona could walk, Grandma Concetta took her along when she gathered herbs and weeds for her lotions and potions. Grandma Concetta was a strega, and all the villagers came to her for cures and advice on many things.

"Ah, Nonalina, here is *rosmarino*—rosemary. Very good for growing hair, especially on bald heads. Also excellent as furniture polish.

"And here is *aglio selvatico*—wild garlic. The only thing for an upset stomach. Come along. Let's see what else we can find."

By the end of their walk, Grandma Concetta's basket would be filled to overflowing.

When little Nona was old enough to go to school, she was sent
to study with the sisters of the convent. There she met little Amelia,
and they became best friends right away. Nona helped Amelia with
her lessons, especially spelling and writing. And Amelia, in turn, loaned
Nona her pretty hair ribbons, even though Nona didn't ask for them.

One day Amelia looked at Nona and said, "We should do something different with your hair." So Amelia curled it.

"Hmm, perhaps the braids *are* better," Amelia said.

Best of all, Nona and Amelia liked to visit Grandma Concetta. While Nona held the big book of spells and Amelia turned the pages, Grandma Concetta always said, "I knew the first time I looked at you, Nona, that one day you would become a strega. But I had no idea I would have *two* little girls to pass my magic down to. I am filled with *contentezza*—contentment."

Nona and Amelia watched Grandma Concetta mix her lotions and potions. They listened as she talked to the villagers about their troubles—headaches, warts, baldness, and other worries—and gave them her remedies, along with good advice.

And after all the villagers had gone back down the hill at the end of the day, Grandma Concetta gave the girls wonderful plates of steaming hot pasta. It appeared from her pasta pot as if by magic, and it tasted so special that Nona and Amelia always asked Grandma Concetta what her secret ingredient was. But Grandma Concetta would only smile and say nothing.

When the girls finished at the *convento,* the convent school, it was decided that they would go to the city and enter the Accademia delle Streghe—the Academy for Stregas—where they would learn the most modern ways to do magic.

Amelia loved the city—the bustle, the noise, and most of all the shopping. And she loved learning to use the Academy's machines and the new, scientific ways to do spells. "Nona," she said, "this is all so much better than the old ways Grandma Concetta uses."

But Nona missed the old spells. She didn't like the city streets, and she longed for walks in the country with Grandma Concetta, whom she missed most of all.

So Nona went home and climbed the hill to Grandma Concetta's house.

"Well, *cara mia*," Grandma Concetta said after hearing Nona's story, "the Accademia is not for everyone. I have a feeling you need to be right here with me."

So Nona began learning to be a strega from the best strega of them all—Grandma Concetta.

She learned how to mix lotions and potions. She turned the pages of the big book for Grandma Concetta. And she watched the way Grandma Concetta treated each villager who walked up the hill to ask for her help.

Every day Nona cleaned and polished Grandma Concetta's pasta pot.
She knew it was magic, but Grandma Concetta never showed her how
to use it. And whenever Nona asked about it, Grandma Concetta always
answered, "There will be time enough, Nona. Now, here's how you make
the lotion to remove warts. . . ."

"Nona! Grandma Concetta! It's Amelia, home for a visit!"

Oh, it was so good to see Amelia again. They all kissed and talked. Amelia talked the most, telling Nona and Grandma Concetta all about the machines at the Academy and the fancy scientific methods she now knew how to use.

"Did you learn any of the old spells?" Grandma Concetta asked.

"Oh, yes indeed," Amelia answered. "Watch the goat!" She opened her notebook and chanted some strange words: *capra*—goat; *tetto*—roof; and presto! With a bang and a cloud of smoke, Grandma's goat was on the roof!

"*Ecco fatto*—that's it," she exclaimed proudly. "It's a spell for Moving Things Up. We use it to put things back on shelves. Isn't that wonderful?"

"Very good, Amelia. Now will you get my goat down?" Grandma Concetta asked. Amelia looked through her notebook. She looked and looked. "I must have gone shopping that day," she said.

"Maybe Nona can do it," Grandma Concetta said.

Nona looked up at the roof. Then she ran into the house and came back with a bottle of olive oil. She climbed up the tree next to the little house and poured some oil on the roof. The goat slipped and slid right off!

"Oh, Nona, how marvelously clever you are," Amelia said. "But look what I have from the Academy." She opened her *borsa*—purse—and pulled out a big piece of parchment. "This is my diploma that says I am a genuine strega. Now, don't worry, Grandma Concetta, Nona. I'm not going to give you any competition," she said, laughing at her own joke. "But I am opening up business in the town on the other side of the mountain. It's much bigger and busier than our little village. And it has so many shops! You must come and see me," she told them. "Well, I'm off. *Arrivederci*, sweet Nona, sweet Grandma Concetta."

That evening, Nona and Grandma Concetta sat outside before Nona went home. Nona was very quiet.

"Nonalina, *cara*," Grandma Concetta said, "what is the matter?"

"I guess I'll never be a real strega like Amelia. I won't ever have a diploma."

"Ah," Grandma Concetta said, "you don't need a diploma to be a true strega. You already have everything you need. You have the spirit and kindness that come from the heart. And when I pass my practice over to you, I will tell you the *ingrediente segreto*—the secret ingredient. Then you will be not only a true strega, but a great one."

Years went by. One day, Grandma Concetta called Nona to her. "It's time, Nona. I am ready to retire. I am going to spend the rest of my days at the seashore, and you must take my place. You shall have my little house, my book of spells, my herbs, and my remedies.

"And in the cupboard, I have left you my pasta pot with something inside it." And with that Grandma Concetta said, "From this day forth, you shall be known as Strega Nona!"

Then she put on her cloak, picked up her bag, and started down the hill.

Nona stood in front of the little house that was now hers. She waved and waved until Grandma Concetta was out of sight. Nona wiped away a tear and walked inside. She went straight to the cupboard and looked in the pasta pot. There she found a letter.

Cara Strega Nona,

my magic pasta pot is now yours.
Whenever you are hungry, sing the
little song written here, and the pot
will bubble and boil and fill with
fresh hot pasta. When you have
enough, sing the second song.

But then you MUST blow three kisses
and the pot will stop.

For that is the INGREDIENTE SEGRETO,
LOVE...
It is the same with all your magic.
Always LOVE!

Your Grandma Concetta

①

BUBBLE BUBBLE PASTA POT,
BOIL ME SOME PASTA,
  NICE AND HOT,
I'M HUNGRY AND IT'S
  TIME TO SUP.
BOIL ENOUGH PASTA
  TO FILL ME UP.

②

ENOUGH, ENOUGH PASTA POT,
I HAVE MY PASTA,
  NICE AND HOT.
SO SIMMER DOWN
  MY POT OF CLAY,
UNTIL I'M HUNGRY
  ANOTHER DAY.

More years passed, and Strega Nona was loved by everyone. She helped all the people who came to her with their troubles, even the priest and the sisters of the convent. She did have a magic touch.

And always, Strega Nona never forgot the *ingrediente segreto*.

Life was happy in the little house on the hill. Strega Nona kept the goat, a peacock, a rabbit, and a dove for company.

But Strega Nona was getting old, and she needed someone to help keep her little house and garden and her dear animals. So she went down to the village square and put up a sign.

The next day there was a knock on her door.

The rest is history.